WELCOME TO RAVENS PASS

LOST ISLAND

by Steve Brezenoff
illustrated by Amerigo Pinelli

Ravens Pass is published by Stone Arch Books
a Capstone imprint
1710 Roe Crest Drive
North Mankato, Minnesota 56003
www.capstonepub.com

Cataloging-in-Publication Data is available at the Library of Congress website.
ISBN: 978-1-4342-4614-1 (library binding)
ISBN: 978-1-4342-6214-1 (paperback)

Summary: Two boys wreck their boat on a creepy island and it seems to hold mysteries.

Graphic Designer: Hilary Wacholz
Art Director: Kay Fraser

Photo credits:
iStockphoto: chromatika (sign, back cover); spxChrome (torn paper, pp. 7, 17, 23, 33, 39, 45, 53, 61, 67, 73, 83)
Shutterstock: Milos Luzanin (newspaper, pp. 92, 93, 94, 95, 96); Robyn Mackenzie (torn ad, pp. 1, 2, 96); Tischenko Irina (sign, pp. 1, 2).

Printed in China by Nordica
0514/CA21400798
052014   008217R

Between where you live and where you've been, there is a town. It lies along the highway, and off the beaten path. It's in the middle of a forest, and in the middle of a desert. It's on the shore of a lake, and along a raging river. It's surrounded by mountains, and on the edge of a deadly cliff. If you're looking for it, you'll never find it, but if you're lost, it'll appear on your path.

The town is **RAVENS PASS,** and you might never leave.

TABLE OF CONTENTS

Chapter 1

THE RIVER

The sun was just sneaking up from the hills behind Ravens Pass. Garrett Plume tossed two life jackets into his rowboat. It was tricky, because he wore an ACE bandage on his right elbow. He'd broken his arm at the start of summer in a boating accident with his best friend, Henry Mortus.

This would be their first time back on the boat and on the river since the accident.

Garrett checked his watch and sighed. In the cool morning air, he could see his breath.

"Morning, Garrett," said Henry as he walked up. He wore a bandage on his arm too, identical to Garrett's.

"How's your arm today?" Garrett asked.

Henry shrugged. "Same as yours, probably," he said. He didn't smile.

Ever since the boating accident, Garrett had noticed Henry hadn't been smiling much, if at all. Now that they both had their hard casts off, though, Garrett was hoping Henry might cheer up a little. That's why he'd suggested they head out nice and early for a rowboat ride — nothing like the high-speed adventure that broke both their arms earlier in the summer.

Garrett tossed a tackle box and two fishing rods into the boat. "I'm not sure we'll be able to cast too well," he said, "but it's worth a try."

Henry nodded. "I guess so," he said.

Garrett put his hands on his hips. "All right," he said. "Climb aboard. I'll push us off." He pulled off his sneakers, then his socks, and tossed them into the boat. Then he rolled up his jeans.

Henry stepped into the boat and sat in the stern. Then Garrett leaned heavily on the bow and, with a grunt, pushed the boat off the beach. He jogged alongside for a few steps, then hopped in. The rowing hurt his sore arm at first, but after a few strokes, it actually felt pretty good.

Garrett smiled. The river through Ravens Pass was calm that morning. Rowing was easy. In a few minutes he'd found a nice quiet spot to drop his line. He started baiting his hook.

"Hey," Garrett said as he worked, "how about some lemonade?"

"Oh," Henry said. "I forgot to bring any."

"You didn't bring anything?" Garrett asked. "You were supposed to bring sandwiches for lunch, too."

Henry shrugged and stared out over the water.

Garrett took a deep breath and sighed. It was getting harder to give Henry a break for moments like this. Ever since the accident, it was like Henry was only half there — the rest of him was still under the overturned sailboat, struggling against the raging foam of the river, just trying to stay alive.

"Look at that," Henry said.

Before Garrett even looked up from his hook, a chilly wind blew across his hunched shoulders. He couldn't see the hook anymore — not well enough to bait it — because it had grown suddenly dark.

He looked out across the river. Ravens Pass looked like a model on the horizon. A gang of heavy low clouds moved toward them.

"Uh-oh," Garrett said. He dropped his fishing rod and grabbed both oars. "We'd better get back, pronto."

Henry didn't seem to hear him. He kept watching the storm roll toward them. "Looks just like the one that got us, huh?" he said.

Garrett nodded as he rowed madly.

He remembered that stormy morning. The weather report had been good. The boys hadn't had anything to fear. But a big thunderstorm shifted and arrived at Ravens Pass, almost without warning. The boys hadn't had time to get back to shore before the storm hit.

"This time," Garrett said between puffs of breath, "at least we won't capsize."

Henry looked at Garrett then, shaking his head slowly. And at that instant, the storm crashed down. Fear rose in Garrett's chest, but he glanced at Henry and knew he couldn't let them have another accident.

Lightning struck, and thunder clapped in Garrett's ears, as loud as anything. The rain fell in buckets, and in an instant both boys were soaked to the skin. Before long, the rowboat was filling with rainwater.

Garrett rowed even harder, but with every stroke, the water just rose higher in the boat. "We'll never make it to shore!" he shouted over the din.

It was happening again.

Garrett grabbed a life jacket and slipped it over his head. Then he tossed the other to Henry. "Put it on!" he shouted.

Henry did, and just in time. The river grew wild, and soon it churned and foamed like the ocean against a cliff wall. The swelling river lifted the rowboat and tossed it. It was upside down, and then the boys were both tossed into the raging river.

Chapter 2
WASHED ASHORE

Garrett's arm was throbbing. He woke up with his face in the sand and sat up. He held his arm with the other hand and groaned. His bandage was torn and drenched. He pulled it off — it only hung loosely — and tossed it into the sand.

It was sunny now, and he had to squint as he sat up. He looked out over the river.

"It's calm now," he said. "What a weird storm."

"Here," Henry said.

Garrett looked up. His friend stood over him, holding his hand out to help him up. Garrett took it and got up. Henry's bandage was gone, probably lost in the rushing river someplace.

"Boat's gone," Henry said. He crossed his arms and looked around. "Must have washed up someplace else."

"Unless it sank," Garrett said.

"Or that," Henry admitted.

He looked around. The beach was narrow and curved away from him in both directions. He figured they'd washed up on an island or a peninsula, but he couldn't imagine how an island this size could sit in the little river that ran through Ravens Pass.

Maybe they'd floated farther than he thought.

Garrett took a few steps to check his legs. They were a little sore, but they seemed okay. He could walk, anyway.

"Where do you think we are?" Garrett asked. "I can't figure it out."

Henry shrugged. "Looks like an island," he said, looking at the woods behind him. "We can split up and walk along the shore. We might find the boat quicker that way."

Garrett gave him a sharp look. "Split up?" he said. "You're nuts."

Henry squinted at him. "It'd be quicker," he said.

Garrett shook his head. "No way," he said. "We stick together. I don't even know how far we floated. We could be anywhere."

"Okay," Henry said. "Which way should we start looking?"

Garrett watched the river. It lapped against the beach gently. He had a hunch heading left would be the best bet. "This way," he said. And they started walking.

Chapter 3

A TREE

"It's getting hot," Garrett said after they'd been walking for a while.

Henry mumbled in agreement. But he didn't look tired, and he didn't wipe the back of his hand across his forehead.

Garrett did, over and over, and still he sweated and wished he had a bottle of water.

"I wish you'd remembered the lemonades and sandwiches," Garrett said.

"They would have been lost in the river anyway," Henry pointed out.

"Maybe it's not an island," Garrett said. "It doesn't make any sense."

"Maybe," said Henry. "But I think it is."

"Then this can't be the river anymore," Garrett insisted.

"Maybe it gets very wide in some places," Henry said.

Garrett glanced at his friend. "Maybe," he said, but he didn't think it was even possible.

This couldn't be an island. It seemed like the shore of a big lake. Maybe even an ocean.

"Ugh. We've been walking forever," Garrett said.

"Not forever," Henry said. He slipped his hands into the pockets of his jeans. "Forever is a really long time."

"It's just an expression," Garrett started to say. "You know —"

Then, on his left, something creaked in the woods. "Did you hear that?" he asked in a whisper. He stopped short and grabbed Henry's elbow to stop him, too.

Henry shook his head. "I didn't hear anything," he said. "Keep walking."

Garrett ignored his friend and took a step toward the woods. As he did, the creaking grew louder and then something snapped.

It was as loud and frightening as the first clap of thunder from the storm.

Garrett looked up at the tall trees at the edge of the woods. One of them leaned heavily toward the shore. It was falling — it was falling on him and Henry.

Garrett took five long strides along the beach and looked back at Henry. His friend just stood there, looking up at the big old tree as it fell.

"Watch out!" Garrett shouted. "It's falling!"

But Henry didn't hear him, or else he ignored him. Garrett had to move quickly. He kicked off from the sand, dove at his friend's waist, and knocked him back about ten feet. It was just enough, and it was just in time. The tree slammed into the beach, shaking the ground and sending out a cloud of sand and needles.

Garrett coughed and got up.

He wiped the needles and sand from his shoulders and hair. "Are you nuts?" he snapped, looking down at Henry.

Henry just sat up and looked at the fallen tree. "That was weird," he said.

"I'll say," Garrett said. "It was weird that you didn't jump out of the way!"

Henry looked back at him and Garrett nearly flinched. He realized his friend had hardly looked him in the eye all day. Henry's eyes looked dark and faraway, like they were made of glass — like the eyes of an old-fashioned stuffed animal. They were Henry's, but they weren't.

"Sorry for shouting," Garrett said, though he wasn't. But he was worried about Henry. "I just didn't want you to get squashed by that tree. Not after . . ."

He stopped. Henry turned around and looked at the woods.

"Not after that accident," Henry said, staring into the darkness between the trees.

"We almost died, Henry," Garrett said.

Henry didn't turn around, but his head bobbed in a nod. Neither boy said anything for a few minutes.

Garrett thought about the boating accident — the freak storm, the sailboat flipping over, the mast slamming against his body, and Henry floating on his face above him, his eyes open underwater. Garrett shot up through the water and pulled him to safety.

Another minute in that river, and —

Garrett didn't even want to think about it.

"We'd better go around," Henry said. He started into the woods and Garrett followed.

The fallen tree was quite tall. They came to the roots, upturned from the earth.

"Look at this," Garrett said. He stood next to the fallen tree's roots. "They're all black and rotten." He put a hand on the thick trunk, just north of the roots. "The rest of the tree seems so healthy. I wonder what happened."

Henry didn't answer. He just stared into the woods.

"Look," Garrett said. "It's all black, like it died from the ground up."

Garrett reached out to touch it, to see what the rotted roots felt like. They looked like they would crumble at his touch.

"Stop!" Henry snapped. He grabbed Garrett's wrist. "Don't touch it."

Garrett pulled his hand away. "Why not?" he said, spinning to face Henry. "What's your problem?"

"You shouldn't touch it," Henry said. He was calm again, flat. "Let's get back to the beach."

Garrett grunted, but said, "Okay." He followed Henry around the rotting roots and back up the other side of the trunk toward the treeline.

Both boys stopped short. Between them and the beach, right where the trees met the sand, was a group of people.

Chapter 4
DECAY

There were five or six people standing with their backs to the boys, looking out over the river.

Garrett actually smiled. "Hey," he called out. He started to walk faster. "Wow! I'm so glad to see you!"

The people didn't turn around. They didn't even move.

"Hello?" Garrett said. He slowed down. His smile faded. As he got closer, he noticed their clothes. Their pants were torn, ragged and short, like they'd been here a while.

Garrett whispered over his shoulder to Henry, "I think they must have shipwrecked too. But they look like they've been here for years."

Henry didn't reply, and Garrett walked on. "Can you help us?" he said. "Hello?"

He was only a few feet away now, and the people still didn't even turn around. Garrett reached for the nearest one — he looked to be a boy about his own age. They were about the same height.

He grabbed the boy's shoulder, and finally he turned. Garrett wished he hadn't.

His face was pale, with spots of green and blotches of black and brown. His eyes were sunken, like he hadn't eaten in days. His mouth hung open, and a fuzzy moss seemed to be growing on his lips.

The boy's face was as rotten as the tree roots had been. He moaned and lurched toward Garrett.

Garrett jumped backward, still staring. "Henry," he called out. "What's wrong with —"

But he couldn't finish, because when he turned, he saw Henry.

And Henry's face was rotten too.

Chapter 5

INTO THE WOODS

Garrett didn't even think. He just started running. Deeper and deeper into the woods he ran, his bare feet throbbing with pain as he stepped on rocks and sharp twigs. His ankle twisted and he bit his lip to stop from crying.

But he kept running. He couldn't stop. The image of Henry's face wouldn't leave his mind.

It was unbelievably dark. Sunrise wasn't that long ago, Garrett knew, yet it seemed to be twilight now. Night seemed to creep in quickly under the heavy and thick canopy of the forest.

These thoughts hardly crossed his mind, though, because from behind him he could hear the sound of fast footsteps. He darted and turned, knocking through bushes and into tree trunks. Twice he tripped and landed on the wet leaf-covered ground. But he got up again and ran on, deeper into the darkening woods.

Yet the footsteps kept following, closer and closer, faster and faster. They were steady and firm. They never faltered, never slowed. Whoever they were — maybe the six decaying people from the beach, maybe even Henry — they didn't seem to trip. It was like the woods were their home, and they knew every bump and root and stone.

In the canopy, wind pushed branches and leaves along, so the treetops seemed to move with him. Crows dove and cawed. He felt a wing at his ear, and he screamed.

Garrett's bare foot caught under an exposed root. He tumbled to the wet ground, hard this time, and his knee struck a rock.

He couldn't get up so quickly. His knee throbbed with pain. He bent his leg against his chest and hugged it. He struggled to sit up.

When he did, the footsteps finally stopped. A pair of bare feet appeared beside him. He looked up, and Henry was looking as normal as ever — besides that change in his eyes, the change that came with the boating accident.

"You okay?" Henry asked. He squatted next to Garrett. "Why'd you take off like that?"

Garrett couldn't speak. He just stared at Henry. He nearly reached out and touched his friend's face, to see if it was real, if it would just crumble away like the roots of that tree.

"I guess you freaked out, huh?" Henry said. "I don't blame you. They didn't seem friendly to me, either."

"Who didn't?" Garrett asked in barely a whisper.

Henry thumbed over his shoulder toward the beach.

"Those people on the beach," Henry said. "They seemed unfriendly."

"Unfriendly?" Garrett said in disbelief. "Henry, they seemed dead."

Chapter 6
A LONG TIME

Garrett finally calmed down. It took some doing. Henry had to promise over and over that the people on the shore had looked normal to him.

"You were probably seeing things, Garrett," Henry said. "You're dehydrated, I bet. Also you're exhausted."

Garrett kicked at a clump of dead leaves as they walked. "I guess," he admitted. His mouth was very dry, and his legs were sore. He also still had water from the river in his ears.

"Let's find the shore," Garrett said. "The sooner we're off this island, the better."

Henry looked around. "Which way should we go?" he asked.

"Doesn't matter," Garrett said. He started walking a little faster. "As long as we go in a straight line, we'll have to find the shore eventually."

"Only if this really is an island," Henry said quietly.

The boys walked through the thick woods. The canopy was still thick and dark, so very little sunlight made it to the forest floor.

Neither boy spoke much for several minutes. Garrett was beginning to sweat, and he was very thirsty.

"Hey," Henry said, smiling. "Remember your fifth birthday party?"

"What?" Garrett said. He frowned and glanced at his friend.

"Remember?" Henry went on. "Your mom hired that magician. He must have been a hundred years old."

"Magician?" Garrett said. "What are you talking about? Who cares about my fifth birthday party?"

Henry didn't seem to hear him. He laughed. "Oh, and remember when we went to the water park with our dads?" Henry said. "When was that? Like five years ago?"

"Henry!" Garrett snapped. "I don't feel like talking about that right now. Let's just find the shore."

Henry shook his head, smiling. He chuckled. "My dad flipped the big tube over, remember?" he said. "Oh, man. We got soaked." He elbowed Garrett. "Remember?"

Garrett stopped and faced Henry. "Yes!" he said. "I remember. Why are you thinking about this stuff now? We're lost!"

Henry shrugged and looked at his feet. "I don't know," he said sheepishly. "I was just remembering. We've been friends a long time."

Garrett sighed. "I know," he said.

He tried to be patient. His friend had been through a lot lately.

"But right now, we're lost," Garrett said. "And it's hot, and I'm thirsty. I just want to find our boat and get home."

Henry nodded. "I know," he said. "Sorry."

"It's okay," Garrett said. He punched Henry lightly in the arm.

"Ow," Henry said.

Garrett laughed. "Let's keep moving," he said. And the boys walked on.

Chapter 7

LOST

They walked for hours. The woods didn't end. They just got thicker and darker.

Garrett and Henry crossed a stream. They came to a clearing, briefly, and Garrett even smiled, thinking they'd reached the shore.

But it was just a clearing, and the woods went on in every direction.

"I don't get it," Garrett said. He dropped down in the middle of the clearing to rest.

Henry stood next to him.

"How could it be this big?" Garrett asked.

He looked up at Henry. The sun, past its highest point now, caught his eye. His eyes ran with tears and he squinted.

Henry sat down. "I don't know," he said.

"I mean, it's an island in a river," Garrett said. "And it's not even a very big river. It can't be this big."

"We have been walking a long time," Henry said. "Maybe it's not an island. Or maybe it's not an island like we've ever heard of. You know. Maybe it's some new kind of island."

"There's only one kind of island," Garrett said, shaking his head slowly. "A bit of land surrounded by water. That's an island."

"I guess," Henry said. He picked a few blades of grass and tore them into tiny pieces.

Garrett watched him.

Henry didn't seem sweaty or thirsty. He almost seemed happy. Although, Garrett knew, "happy" wasn't quite the right word.

Henry wasn't smiling, but he seemed peaceful. In fact, for the first time since the accident, he seemed like Henry again.

"How come you're not tired?" Garrett said. He felt angry, but he wasn't sure why. He knew it was silly to be angry because his friend wasn't tired. But he couldn't help it.

"I feel like I'm going to pass out," Garrett snapped. "And if I don't some water soon, I probably will pass out."

Henry shrugged. "I'm just not," he said. "Maybe it's because I've gotten so much rest lately. You know, after the accident."

"Yeah, the accident," Garrett said. He stood up and paced around the clearing. "It's all you ever talk about when I see you. To be honest, I'm tired of talking about it. That's all we talk about."

Henry squinted up at Garrett.

"Of course, I hardly ever see you," Garrett said. "I've hardly seen you all summer. And school starts soon."

Henry didn't answer. He stared off into the woods.

"The sun's going down," Garrett said. "We've been here all day."

"Yeah," Henry said.

"Our parents are probably worried," Garrett said.

He looked at the sun. It would set soon.

"Come on," he said. "We have to find some firewood or something. It'll start getting cold once the sun is down."

"We're staying?" Henry said. "I mean, you can't camp out here, can you? You need water and food."

Garrett scratched his chin. "I don't think we have a choice," he said. "Come on." He headed to the edge of the woods.

Chapter 8
FIRELIGHT

The fire started easily. Henry piled the twigs and branches into a pyramid shape. Somehow he got a spark off a couple of rocks. Before Garrett knew it, the fire was big and blazing.

"That was pretty amazing," Garrett said.

"I guess I was paying attention in our outdoor club meetings," Henry replied with a smile. "Remember outdoor club?"

"Not the reminiscing again!" Garrett said. He laughed. "We have been friends a long time, huh?"

Henry nodded, but he looked sad. Garrett was going to ask him what was wrong, but something snapped in the woods.

"What was that?" Garrett said. He spun to face the trees, but he couldn't see anything.

"I think it was just the fire popping," Henry said. "Don't worry about it."

It was very dark now. Only the clearing was bright, lit by their fire and some early moonlight. Something rustled at the edge of the clearing.

"There it is again," Garrett said. He took a step toward the clearing. "Didn't you hear it?"

Henry didn't move. He just sat facing the fire, staring at the jumping flames and sparks.

Garrett grunted and stomped toward the edge of the clearing.

"Who's there?" Garrett shouted.

As if in response, the trees began to shake and the undergrowth wiggled.

Dark figures stepped out of the woods: dozens of them, all unfamiliar and bathed in shadow. They stood just inside the clearing and watched Henry and Garrett.

Garrett backed closer to the fire, until the back of his legs knocked into Henry's back. He watched as the figures moved a little closer.

He could barely tell they were moving. In fact, they didn't seem to move at all, but every time he looked from one to another, they seemed a little closer.

It was like the clearing itself was getting smaller.

Garrett could see their faces now, just a little, and their clothes. They were tattered and torn — their faces and their clothes. Their eyes were deep and black. None wore shoes. None smiled. None spoke. They just stared with deep and dead eyes.

Chapter 9

THE GHOSTS

"Henry," Garrett whispered urgently. "They're everywhere. They've surrounded us."

"I know," Henry said. He still didn't move or look up. He just stared into the fire.

"You don't seem worried," Garrett said.

"I'm not," Henry said. "I don't think they're going to hurt us."

Garrett glanced down at Henry. Then he faced the woods. He summoned all his courage.

"Hey!" Garrett shouted at the strange figures. He was sure they were ghosts. "What do you want with us?"

They didn't reply. They didn't flinch.

"We're getting out of here," Garrett said. He grabbed a log from the edge of the fire. It was cold at one end and flaming at the other. "Come on."

Garrett grabbed Henry by the elbow and pulled him to his feet. Then, waving the flaming log in front of him, he stomped toward the edge of the clearing.

"Move aside!" he said as he walked. The figures finally moved. They covered their ghoulish faces with their arms and hands. They wailed and moaned as if the fire was burning them, even from yards away.

Garrett waved the log. "Move!" he shouted. But as the bright light from his torch fell on each dead face, the figures vanished before his eyes. When he moved the log away, they reappeared.

"Ghosts," Garrett whispered.

"Yes," Henry said.

Garrett took a deep breath and threw the burning log at the specters. It fell at the feet of two of them, and those two vanished.

"Let's go," Garrett said. "This way!"

He dove through the gap in the circle of ghosts, back into the woods.

Henry called to him: "Wait!" but Garrett didn't stop.

He could barely see. If it had been dark during daylight, the night was positively black.

He tripped and stumbled on roots and stones. He knocked his shoulder and arms against the trunks of trees, over and over. He knew he'd be bruised. He didn't care. He had to get away. He had to the find the boat and leave this terrible island.

Chapter 10

LETTING GO

"Hurry, Henry!" Garrett shouted as he ran. He could hear his friend's footsteps behind him — if they were his friend's. Maybe they were the footsteps of the ghosts.

But whenever Garrett found a sliver of moonlight — the tiniest light that somehow broke through the canopy — there would be Henry, running next to him.

When the moonlight was gone, Henry was gone too.

"Where are you?" Garrett called into the darkness.

"I'm here," Henry called back. His voice sounded far away and dim.

Garrett ran on. His toes and feet ached and burned with a hundred little cuts and bruises. His arm was sore where it had been broken. His chest throbbed from lack of breath. His head spun and swam, begging for water.

And suddenly, the woods ended. Garrett tumbled through the underbrush and landed face first on sand.

"The shore," he mumbled, getting to his feet. "I've found the shore."

The river water lapped against the beach in the moonlight.

The rowboat was half on the sand. Both oars were still in their oarlocks. Somehow they had survived the white water and capsize. Somehow the boat was righted, and empty of water, ready to use.

Garrett crawled to the boat. He almost didn't believe his eyes. He put his hands on the edge of the boat and felt the wood and metal.

It was real.

"Henry!" Garrett shouted over his shoulder. "I've found the boat."

There was no reply.

"Henry!" Garrett shouted again.

He turned to face the woods, and there was his friend, standing at the edge of the beach, his bare feet not quite on the sand.

Henry's pants and shirt were tattered and dirty and torn. His face was gaunt and tired. But he smiled. It was a small smile, a sad smile.

"I've found the boat," Garrett said. He smiled too, an open-mouth grin. "What are you waiting for?"

Henry didn't step forward. He put his hands into the pockets of his torn-up jeans.

"They're coming, Henry!" Garrett shouted. "The ghosts. They're coming. They're coming for you!"

"I know," Henry replied.

"Come with me!" Garrett snapped. "I won't let them take you!"

Henry was upset now, no longer smiling. To Garrett's surprise, he realized Henry was crying.

His mind flashed back to the beginning of the summer, to the accident. He remembered Henry's face above him, floating in the cold river water.

He remembered afterward, lying in bed at the hospital, asking about Henry.

"Is he okay?" he'd asked. But no one would answer.

Now Garrett looked at his friend at the edge of the woods. He screamed, "Come with me!"

"You know I can't, Garrett," Henry said. His voice was calm and warm. "It's time for you to leave me here."

"But . . ." Garrett said. His voice trailed off, but he suddenly felt calm. Everything was clear. "I don't want to."

Henry smiled. "I know," he said.

This was where Henry belonged now. This was where he should have been all summer, ever since the accident.

"I'm sorry," Garrett said. "I'm sorry I held you back for so long."

"It's okay," Henry said. "I didn't mind. But now I have to stay here. It's not so bad. I kind of like it here, actually."

The boys stood there like that, under the moonlight, looking at each other. As they did, the moon grew brighter and higher in the sky. The other ghosts from the island gathered at the edge of the beach. Now they, too, seemed to be smiling. They closed in around Henry.

"I guess I'll see you," Garrett said. "Some day." He climbed into the rowboat and sat down.

"Not for a very long time," Henry called back.

Garrett pushed off from the beach. As he rowed along the calm river back toward town, he kept his eyes on his friend. But the farther his boat glided away from the beach, the harder it was to see him. His figure faded and then vanished completely.

Chapter 11

ONE PIECE

Garrett rowed for hours. He fell in and out of sleep. The rowboat seemed to know where to go, so after a long time, Garrett just sat back and let the river guide him home.

He woke up under the rising sun. The boat had landed where he and Henry had pushed off the morning before. The sky over Ravens Pass was orange and yellow.

Garrett stepped off the boat and started for town. As he did, the road in front of him lit up blue and red.

A siren wailed.

The police car pulled up next to him, and Garrett's father jumped out of the passenger seat even before the car had stopped.

"Garrett!" he shouted. He threw his arms around his son.

"I'm okay," he said.

His dad pulled away and looked in Garrett's face. "We've been so worried," he said. "After what happened . . ."

Garrett nodded. He leaned against his dad's chest. "I'm okay," he said. "Now I'm okay."

His father hugged him again.

The policeman climbed out of his car. He called over the open door, "Everyone all right?"

"He's all in one piece," Garrett's dad said, smiling.

"That's a relief," the policeman said.

Garrett looked over his dad's shoulder. He recognized the policeman as the same man who had carried him from the river after the accident.

"Your son's been through a lot this summer," the policeman said. "Let's keep a close eye on him."

Garrett's dad nodded. He said quietly, so only Garrett could hear him, "It's not every summer that you lose your best friend."

ABOUT THE AUTHOR

STEVE BREZENOFF lives in Minneapolis, Minnesota, with his wife, Beth, and their son, Sam. Besides writing books, he enjoys playing video games, riding his bicycle, and helping middle-school students to improve their writing skills. Steve's ideas almost always come to him in his dreams, so he does his best writing in his pajamas.

ABOUT THE ILLUSTRATOR

A long time ago, when AMERIGO PINELLI was very small, his mother gave him a pencil. From that moment on, drawing became his world. Nowadays, Amerigo works as an illustrator above the narrow streets and churches of Naples, Italy. He loves his job because it feels more like play than work. And each morning, as the sun rises over Mount Vesuvius, Amerigo gets to chase pigeons along the rooftops. Just ask his lovely wife, Giulia, if you don't believe him.

GLOSSARY

CANOPY (KAN-uh-pee)—the cover over something, especially the top tree cover of a forest

CAPSIZE (KAP-size)—if a boat or ship capsizes, it flips over in the water

DECAY (di-KAY)—to rot or break down

PENINSULA (puh-NIN-suh-luh)—a piece of land that sticks out from a larger land mass that is surrounded by water

REMINISCING (rem-uh-NISS-ing)—to think or talk about the past and things that you remember

SHEEPISHLY (SHEEP-ish-lee)—meekly or shyly

SPECTERS (SPEK-turz)—ghosts or spirits

TWILIGHT (TWY-lite)—the time of day when the sun has just set and it is beginning to get dark

VANISHED (VAN-ishd)—disappeared

DISCUSSION QUESTIONS

1. Who are the other ghosts on the lost island? What happened to them? Explain your answer.

2. Ravens Pass is a town where crazy things happen. Has anything spooky or creepy ever happened where you live? Talk about scary stories you've heard.

3. Why did Garrett's ghost disappear and reappear at certain times?

WRITING PROMPTS

1. Write a short story from Henry's perspective that explains how he feels when he sees Garrett leave the island.

2. If you could temporarily become a ghost, what would you do? Where would you go? Who would you tell the stories to once you became a normal human again? Talk about it.

3. Why do you think Henry didn't want to tell Garrett that he was a ghost? Write a letter from Henry's point of view.

THE CROW'S

SPECTER OR SPOOF?

Henry Mortus, Ravens Pass resident, has been presumed dead for several months. That is, until Garrett Plume, his former best friend, ran into the young man's ghost on a remote island just outside Ravens Pass.

Yes, you read that right: his GHOST! The Ravens Pass Police Department issued a statement claiming that Garrett's story was likely just a product of trauma resulting from recently losing his best friend. On the surface, that seems like a reasonable explanation. But this reporter decided to dig a little deeper.

A quick boat trip brought me to the remote island. Almost immediately, I spotted several ratty pieces of clothing. I followed them, which led me to a clearing very much like the one Garrett described in the police report. Lastly, as I was leaving, I found what were clearly two sets of footprints leading away from the shore.

So, readers, what do you think? I'll tell you what they want us to think: that Garrett's story is simply a product of his imagination.

But I know that you know better. This is Ravens Pass. Strange and unexplainable things happen here every day, whether we want to believe them or not.

Henry Mortus, the deceased

MORE
DARK TALES

FROM RAVENS PASS